The Magic Egg

Book

By Shauna Nicholson-Kelly

Illustrated by Maris June Findling

The Magic Egg Book
copyright © 2021 Shauna Nicholson-Kelly
First Edition

Hardback ISBN: 978-1-945587-58-0
Paperback ISBN: 978-1-945587-59-7
Library of Congress Control Number: 2020918151
Shauna Nicholson-Kelly
The Magic Egg Book 1. Parenting; 2. Surrogacy; 3. Chickens; 4. Barnyard
Cover and Interior Art: Maris June Findling
Editing and Production: Kim Cooper Findling
Typesetting and Design: Dancing Moon Press

Dancing Moon Press
Bend, Oregon USA
dancingmoonpress.com

DANCING
MOON
PRESS

dedication

For Vaughn, the sweet little baby chick who we wanted more than anything and are grateful for beyond words. We thank God for you every day. The story behind us becoming a family is everything that I have ever wanted. I wouldn't change it or you for anything. I love you.

Jim, you kept me strong when I thought I had nothing left to offer this world. You made me believe again. MALU.

Without you, sweet Sherri, there would be no Vaughn. I'll always love how your sweet children sang and talked to her when she was in your belly.
And to Carly at Baby Bump Journeys; thank you for putting us all together with love and care.

SC, you don't know me yet, but you will soon. Thank you for Vaughn's one dimple. It's everything to me.

LH, my bestie and everyday phone call, thank you for walking with me always.

Mom, we love our Nani and the four months a year you spend with us.

KCF, no book without you, sweetheart.

It was a sunny day on Woodpecker Farm,
and the barnyard was full of excitement.

Inside the big red barn, the hens were happily sitting on their nests.

The mama hens were so excited for their eggs to hatch,
so that they could meet their new baby chicks.

One by one, the eggs cracked apart, and the baby chicks stepped out into the beautiful bright world.

The mama hens and the baby chicks were having so much fun playing and laughing with one another.

The mama hen with the smooth feathers noticed that the hen with the fluffy feathers didn't have a baby chick.

The smooth feathered mama hen walked over to the fluffy feathered hen and asked, "Where is your baby chick?"

The fluffy feathered hen replied, "I don't have any eggs,"
and she quietly walked back into the barn and began to cry.

The smooth feathered mama hen followed the fluffy feathered hen into the barn. "I have many eggs," she said. "You can have one of mine."

The fluffy feathered hen was so happy to have her own egg. She sat on her nest and waited.

While she waited and waited, she watched the chicks play
with the other mamas and she began to feel envious.
Suddenly, her egg turned green.

Then the fluffy feathered hen began to worry about becoming a mama. Would she do a good job? Her egg turned blue with sadness.

The longer the fluffy feathered hen sat, the more excited she became for her baby chick to hatch. Her egg shone orange and yellow with joy.

By the time the egg was nearly ready to hatch, the hen knew she would love her baby chick more than anything in the whole wide world. Her egg glowed red with love.

The very next moment, the egg began to shine
with all of the colors and feelings the fluffy
feathered hen had felt. That is when her egg
became a magic egg.

Then one sunny day on Woodpecker Farm, the fluffy
feathered hen's egg hatched.

The fluffy feathered mama hen finally got to hold her sweet baby chick.

The fluffy feathered mama hen and her new baby chick
scurried out into the barnyard to laugh and play with the
other mama hens and their baby chicks.

While the babies played, the fluffy feathered mama hen found
the smooth feathered mama hen under the walnut tree and
gave her a big hug and said, "Thank you for my amazing gift."

And life went on at Woodpecker Farm, but with just a little more magic than had been there before.

When the baby chick was old enough, the fluffy
feathered mama hen told her the story of her life, and
how one magical day, another mama hen gave her the
gift of an egg for her very own.

And that is how they became a family.

About the Author

Shauna Nicholson-Kelly and her husband Jim Kelly have been married since 2014. They moved from Los Angeles, California to Nashville, Tennessee to raise their daughter, who came to them after years of infertility treatments, a hysterectomy and finally success with a surrogate and donor. This book was created as a way to tell Vaughn her origin story. The author hopes to make an otherwise difficult conversation a little easier for any parents who must explain how their family may have been created differently than other families, but is still just as beautiful.

About the Illustrator

Maris June Findling has been creating art of all kinds since she was a little chick. Now age 13, Maris spends as much time as she possibly can drawing and painting. She also loves sewing, cooking, the forest and the beach. She lives in Bend, Oregon with her family.

DANCING
MOON
PRESS

CPSIA information can be obtained
at www.ICGtesting.com
Printed in the USA
BVHW020804050321
600888BV00007B/12